The
Harvest Queen

Northern Lights Books for Children are published by
Red Deer College Press
56 Avenue & 32 Street Box 5005
Red Deer Alberta Canada T4N 5H5
Edited for the Press by Tim Wynne-Jones
Designed by Kunz + Associates
Printed in Hong Kong for Red Deer College Press
Financial support provided by the Alberta Foundation for the Arts, a beneficiary
of the Lottery Fund of the Government of Alberta, and by the Canada Council,
the Department of Canadian Heritage and Red Deer College.

ALBERTA *Lotteries*   **The Alberta Foundation for the Arts**   **Alberta** COMMUNITY DEVELOPMENT

COMMITTED TO THE DEVELOPMENT OF CULTURE AND THE ARTS

Canadian Cataloguing in Publication Data
Robertson, Joanne, 1946–
The Harvest Queen
(Northern lights books for children)
ISBN 0-88995-134-9
I. Reczuch, Karen. II. Title. III. Series.
PS8585.O3216H37 1996   jC813'.54   C96-910301-8
PZ7.R5465Ha 1996

To my mother, who is a constant source of inspiration. —JR
For Craig and for Kyra, who have also seen fairies dance. —KR

The Harvest Queen

Story by Joanne Robertson
Illustrations by Karen Reczuch

Red Deer College Press

FINALLY! IT'S HERE! HOW CAN anyone sleep?

Out my window, I see the big oak tree in the middle of the garden. Just a skeleton now. Not even one leaf left. And right beside it – a glowing orange jewel. The last pumpkin. Saved for today.

I creep from my covers, careful not to wake Grandma in the guest bed. I get a knife from the kitchen and sneak into the garden in my nightgown. Hacking away, I kidnap the pumpkin from its vine, from its black earth bed. Tiptoeing back into the house, I carry it to my room.

RANDMA'S AWAKE. "BRIGIT," she says, "it's unlucky to keep a pumpkin in your room. Fairy magic may be in it."

Grandma gets out of bed and, in her nightgown, carries the pumpkin back outside.

She says, "We'll build the Harvest Queen after breakfast."

After we eat, we begin. We put a lawn chair under the oak tree. Beside it we stack cornstalks, a pile of wind-dried, sun-bleached bones.

We TWIST VINES FROM BEANS AND peas, tying them around the cornstalks. These long straight arms and straight long legs are tied to a thick and woody sunflower stalk spine. We make muscles of bright autumn leaves.

A braid of garlic tied around the waist holds a skirt of dusty corn leaves. We tighten the belt. Leaves and vines are caught, unable to struggle free. She looks like she has an umbrella in her belly.

Grandma and I lift the headless body and sit it in the chair. We mound mud around her potato feet.

We cut a hole in the bottom of the pumpkin and lift it like a crown, placing it on her sunflower-stalk neck.

"Now she won't lose her head," I laugh.

**We** GIVE HER A CARROT NOSE, CURLY broccoli eyes, and a white pearl onion for the twinkle in her eyes. Two flapping cabbage-leaf ears are held in place by the twisted hair of corn silk and vines.

Her hands rest on her lap. Corncob fingers hold a bouquet made of sunflowers, radishes, spinach leaves, and long red peppers.

"Red is lucky," says Grandma. "It'll be her protection."

From vines of beans and sweet peas with red and yellow flowers, we twist a wreath and place it on her head. I string a necklace of ruby beets and arrange it around her neck.

 ITTING IN HER CHAIR, SHE smiles at us with her purply-white cauliflower teeth.

"Her name is Carlin." Grandma says she's the Harvest Queen.

There's a tale told of how the fairies come to dance with Carlin when they gather their harvest. They're invisible. Only someone wearing a four-leaf clover can see them.

"But, Brigit, if you ever see the fairies, never enter their fairy ring. They'll think you're one of them and try to take you home."

Carlin sits in the dying afternoon light. Grandma goes in the house. I search the garden for a magical four-leaf clover.

Minutes pass – or is it hours? The rising moon is a
ghostly lantern trapped by the long fingers of the old oak
tree. The air shimmers with silver light. Tiny seeds float
down, then suddenly swirl as if caught in a whirlpool.

Shadowy shapes in the silver fog become solid. Fairies! Some small as a leaf, wearing blue heather-bell caps. Others larger, almost as big as Carlin. The air fills with music from straw whistles and twig flutes.

 RUN TO CARLIN. HER HAIR IS blowing in the breeze. No. Not blowing. Growing! Green tendrils poke through the twisted vines. They sway in time to the music.

More tendrils grow, covering her in a mossy-green gown. Green fingernails curl from her dry corncob fingers. Toenails sprout from potato toes.

A curly-haired boy with a horn of plenty tied to his back
approaches Carlin. He holds out his hand. She reaches
for it. Then Carlin stands! She lifts her feet out of the
ground. The fairies swirl around Carlin and the boy.

They dance. The Harvest Queen and the curly-haired
boy. Spinning, twirling, whirling. Flowers burst into
bloom wherever Carlin steps. Seeds burst from the flowers
and cover the garden. Carlin's skirts billow around her,
spreading the seeds, the flowers, the fruit.

Carlin dances in the fragrant living garden. The fairies
follow Carlin, gathering their harvest, filling their horns
of plenty.

 **T**HE CORNUCOPIA OVERFLOWS. Then the boy leads Carlin back to her chair and she collapses into it. The garden begins to die. The music grows slower and quieter. The fairies join hands and form a circle. They sway together and a green fairy ring sprouts under their feet.

Trapping me!

 **T**HE WORDLESS MUSIC ENDS. The fairies stand. Motionless. All stare at me. Silent.

I lift the ruby-red jewels from Carlin's neck and place them around mine. I take the bouquet from her hand. I sit on the ground at Carlin's feet and arrange her dry skirts like a cape around my shoulders.

The boy walks slowly toward me, his hand held out. I hold up the bouquet.

It spins out of my hand, toward his. The red peppers and radishes twist free. Spinning and twirling and whirling, they enclose Carlin and me in glowing red rings. I feel the warmth of the jewels around my neck.

The boy turns, clutching the remains of the bouquet. Fading, he walks to the edge of the fairy ring. The fairies disappear. The red peppers and radishes fall to the ground.

T HE COOL BREEZE BLOWS LEAVES and dust, covering the fairy ring. The moon, escaping from the oak tree's clutches, washes a gold light over the garden.

I get up. I give the necklace back to Carlin and straighten the wreath on her head. I gather the peppers and radishes and place them in her lap. Then I leave her sitting alone in her garden.

**T**HE LIGHTS IN THE KITCHEN are on. I go in. Mom and Grandma are making salad at the table.

"Go get washed, Brigit," says Mom. "Supper's ready."

In my room, I take the four-leaf clover out of my pocket and put it between the pages of a book. When it's dry, I'll ask Grandma to make it into a pendant.

Just like Mom's.